STAR EATERS

BROOKE CARTER

T0243253

ORCA
ANCHOR

ORCA BOOK PUBLISHERS

Published in Canada and the United States
in 2023 by Orca Book Publishers.
orcabook.com

Library and Archives Canada Cataloguing in Publication
Title: Star eaters / Brooke Carter.
Names: Carter, Brooke, 1977- author.
Description: Series statement: Orca anchor
Identifiers: Canadiana (print) 20220185166 | Canadiana (ebook) 20220185182 |
ISBN 9781459834675 (softcover) | ISBN 9781459834682 (PDF) |
ISBN 9781459834699 (EPUB)
Classification: LCC PS8605.A77776 S73 2023 | DDC jC813/.6—dc23

Library of Congress Control Number: 2022934604

Summary: In this high-interest accessible novel for teen readers,
a teen discovers a stowaway on his spaceship designed to
seek out new energy sources.

Orca Book Publishers is committed to reducing the consumption of
nonrenewable resources in the production of our books. We make
every effort to use materials that support a sustainable future.

Orca Book Publishers gratefully acknowledges the support
for its publishing programs provided by the following agencies:
the Government of Canada, the Canada Council for the Arts and
the Province of British Columbia through the BC Arts Council
and the Book Publishing Tax Credit.

Edited by Tanya Trafford
Design by Ella Collier
Cover photography by Getty Images/Artur Debat
and Getty Images/Westend61
Author photo by Laura Housden

Printed and bound in Canada.

26 25 24 23 • 1 2 3 4

For my kids. You are the greatest wish I ever made.

Chapter One

"What world is this?" Destin said. He had been talking to himself more and more. He hadn't seen anyone else in a long time. He was all alone, and there wasn't anyone on this planet. His scans had turned up no life forms.

He stood on the loading ramp of his small starship. He stared in wonder at the land.

This planet was green and lush. Trees and grass and flowers sprang up all over. There was a large lake with bright blue water. And mountains with real snow on them.

"Epic," Destin said.

What world, what kingdom, what shores? Words floated in his mind. They were bits and pieces of old books he'd read. He'd found the books stashed in a locker at his bunk. Whoever had used the ship before Destin had left them there. The IRIS Corp, his owners, did not allow him to own books. They didn't like their fleet knowing too much. So Destin had only ever read books about flying and tech and star maps. He could get in a lot of trouble for having the old books. But this was a one-pilot starship, made to carry only one Raider. It wasn't that hard for Destin to hide them.

Raider, Destin thought. How he hated the name IRIS had given young pilots like him. It was a Raider's job to search the galaxy for energy to steal from distant stars. The best energy came from the suns of small planets. Their energy could be "taken" by the Star Eater tech on board a Raider's ship. A small sun could fill the energy cells all the way up, so Destin would only have to make one trip. He'd steal the energy and then carry it back to base. Done.

IRIS didn't like it when their Raiders went off course. And they *really* didn't like it when Raiders left airspace to visit planets. Destin was never supposed to set foot on the ground. He was trained to stay on his ship at all times. All IRIS cared about was the energy. They didn't care about Destin. He could die out in space and they'd just replace him.

But he'd still decided to break all the rules and visit this planet. What kind of danger was out there in the green trees? It was unsafe enough to land, but to stand there with the door open? Very risky. He wasn't even sure what he'd meant to do. Take a peek? But then he'd seen how pretty it was.

It was a land he'd only ever seen on screens or in his dreams. And the *light*. The sunlight shone down over everything. It was this light that made him walk to the edge of the ramp. His toes were inches from the ground.

Destin took a deep breath and stepped forward. And that was it. He'd done it. He was standing on a strange planet. In the sun. He turned his face to the sky. It was so warm. And so bright! When he looked away, tiny orbs of light danced in front of his eyes.

He'd trained to eat suns since he was a small child. He'd flown short missions since he was fifteen. And now he was a pilot of his own Raider ship at seventeen. But he'd never felt the warmth of a real sun on his face.

He walked a few more steps away from his ship and felt a warm breeze rush past him.

He knew he could get into a lot of trouble for this, so he had to cover his tracks. He turned his nav system off so the stop wouldn't show up on his flight log. He loved hand flying anyway.

The beeper on his wrist chimed. Spirals of red were spinning down. They showed the status of his ship's Star Eater energy cells. They were getting too low. He was going to have to steal this warm sun away from this beautiful planet. It was the last thing he wanted to do.

The beeper chimed again. The sound would only repeat, faster and faster, until he did something about it. He didn't have much time. Destin sighed and took one last look at the pretty planet before walking back into the cold steel of his ship.

He sat in the pilot chair and spun around to the helm. He checked his systems. Energy was in the red zone—too low—but the Star

Eater was ready to launch. He closed the doors and sealed off the hull and then lifted off. He shot straight up into the sky and watched as the green and blue got farther away. Soon he was back in the dark of space, with the planet below him.

Destin was about to bring the nav system back online when he saw his comms screen blinking.

"Oh no," Destin said. His voice was a lonely sound in the empty ship. "Three missed hails. Destin, you fool."

IRIS had tried to hail him while he was off looking at the planet's surface. With a shaking hand he pressed the *comms* button.

There was a trill as the call went through. Then the tight face of his boss, Captain Juno, flashed on the screen. She did not look happy. This was bad. Captain Juno was a scary woman. She cared about nothing but the energy.

"Raider 1984-225, you have not answered your comms. Report at once," Juno said.

"I...I...was fixing some bugs on my system," Destin said, coming up with a quick lie. "I'm sorry. It won't happen again."

Juno frowned. "What is your current status, Destin X?"

She had called him by his name. Destin wasn't sure if that was good or bad. All the other kids like him—ones raised by IRIS to fly Star Eaters—were called X. No last names. No history. No parents. No families. And no way to trace a Raider as they went missing on missions or in "accidents" at the training hub.

Destin swallowed. His throat was so dry. "I am almost done my mission," he said. "I found a good star. I will be returning to base soon."

Juno leaned toward the comms screen. "IRIS needs the energy, Destin X," she said.

"I understand," said Destin. "I'll get it."

"Be sure that you do," said Juno. "You are a new Raider. IRIS needs you to work hard. If you don't, we will have to pull you. And…send you back to the hub."

Destin's heart began to pound so hard that he thought Juno would hear it from across the galaxy. He nodded. "I…understand." Not the hub. No way. Anything but the hub.

With that, the hail link ended and the screen went blank.

"I have to steal this sun," he said. He started the Star Eater sequence but paused before hitting the final command button. His fingers shook. He didn't want to hurt the planet. But he had to, didn't he?

Chapter Two

"Push the button," he said. "Just push it and do your job. Or someone else will." His finger hovered over the large green button on his control panel.

Destin knew that if he stole the energy from the sun, it would die. And that meant the planet would die too. It would freeze over and turn to ice.

Juno's threat about sending him back to the hub had hit him hard. That scared him more than anything. He couldn't give up his Raider ship. Because the only thing worse than being alone was living in the hub. He'd rather die than go back there.

So he pushed the button.

The Star Eater tech rumbled as it reached out from his ship on a long robot arm. At the end was a large round dome that unfolded. It looked like a huge flower opening up to the sun. In the middle of it was a dark spot that looked like an eye. It grew and shrank and seemed to focus like an eye too. The dark spot in the middle gave Destin chills. It was the thing that sucked every bit of life from a sun. It was always hungry for energy.

It would eat up everything and then store it in the big power cells on his ship.

The Star Eater whined as it powered up. Rays of light shot from the sun toward the Star Eater as the tech took all the energy it could. Soon the energy cells were up to max, and his ship hummed with power. The Star Eater pulled back. It folded up its long arm, and Destin was happy to see it done. Now to return to base.

He looked out the window at the planet. It was still alive for now. The energy he'd taken wasn't enough to kill the bright sun yet, but it had dimmed. It wouldn't be long before the planet died.

He sighed. "Goodbye, pretty planet," he said. "I'm sorry."

Destin entered in a comms message. "This is Raider 1984-225, Destin X. I have full-power-cell status. Coming back to base now."

He was about to hit *enter* when he heard a soft sound behind him. It sounded like someone had said, "No."

He spun around in his chair. There was a person. A girl. On his ship. She was crying, shaking.

And she was not supposed to be there.

Chapter Three

"Who are you?" Destin yelled. He leaped from his chair. "What do you want?"

The girl was short, with pale hair and tanned skin. She looked to be about his age. It was hard to tell because most kids he knew from the hub didn't eat well. She seemed healthy, with a full face and strong-looking arms and legs.

"What's your ID number?" he asked. But was she even from the hub? Had she been on his ship the whole time? How could he not have seen her? He noticed she was wearing soft, light clothes. Nothing like the scratchy IRIS clothing he wore.

The girl didn't answer. Destin had a very bad feeling about this.

"What sector are you from?"

She shook her head, still crying. She pointed to the window. "Home," she said. "What have you done to my home?"

"Your…home?" Destin felt panic in his chest. Oh no, he thought, this is why they say you shouldn't go down to the surface.

She could be anyone. She could do anything! He was going to be in so much trouble. IRIS would send him back to the hub for sure. This couldn't be happening.

"I have to get you off the ship," he said. "I don't know who you are, but you can't be here. I must take you back to the surface."

"H-how?" she said. "You're killing my planet. You have to put it back."

"Put it back?" Destin felt like laughing and crying at the same time. "That's not going to happen. I mean, it's way too dangerous. And even if I could do it, I can't. Because they'll send me back to..." He didn't want to say it out loud.

"No," he said. "I'm sorry, whoever you are, but no."

She strode toward him. He jumped back and smashed into the control panel.

"Ow!" he cried. "Stay back!"

"Please," she said. "My home. My people. You are…a Star Eater? We've heard of you. We always feared you would come. We don't have these machines you have. Please pick another planet. Please."

"Look," he said. "It's too late. It won't matter. Even if I put it back, which I can't do, another Raider will just come and take it again."

She cried harder. "Why?" she asked. "Why do this?"

Destin shook his head. "I…have to," he said. "I don't have a choice."

She frowned, but there was something in her golden-brown eyes that seemed to understand.

"IRIS, right?" she said. "They are ruthless."

"Who are you?" Destin asked again. "I thought your planet was empty. My scans showed no people, and you can talk in Uni-speak. I thought...I thought all the allied planets were killed in the wars. I haven't met anyone who knows Uni in a long time— outside the hub, I mean."

After many long wars, and thousands of children taken from other planets, IRIS had said there was no one left alive. Destin didn't know where his home planet was. He didn't even know what to call it or what his name used to be. He only knew that his home no longer existed. Any family he had was long dead.

"You don't know everything," the girl said. "Maybe your scans are wrong for a reason. IRIS doesn't want you to know the truth."

A cold chill went up his spine. Though he did not trust IRIS, he'd never thought his scan tech could be…rigged. Did IRIS do that so he wouldn't see life forms on the planets he killed? It made sense. IRIS didn't care about people. Only energy. Destin was proof of that. But it didn't matter. He couldn't do what this girl was asking.

"You could be right," he said. "But it doesn't matter. Here we are. I'm trapped, and now so are you. I can't put the energy back, and I can't take you with me. So you have to go back down to the surface."

The girl's eyes grew wider. She stared at him like she was looking deep inside his soul. His chest clenched and he felt a ball in his throat, like he was going to cry. What was happening? He felt all this pain rushing through him. He wanted it to stop.

"I'm sick of all this," he said. "I don't want to harm the planets. I love them. And until today I had never even stood on one. But if I don't take the energy back to IRIS, they will come after me. And when they find me they will take away my ship and send me to a place I swore I'd never go back to. So you have to go back. Whoever you are."

The girl took a breath. "My name is Calla," she said.

Destin stared at her. It was a lovely name. Perfect for a person from such a beautiful planet. There was something about her. Something odd but nice. "I'm Destin," he said.

"Destin," she said, "can you hide this from IRIS? Pretend it never happened? You give me back my sun, I go home, and you…go wherever you want."

He shook his head. "You don't get it. There's a tracking beacon."

"Then turn it off," she said.

"I can't. It's the ship itself. As long as it's flying, they can find me. And I'm running out of time."

Destin took the flight controls in his hands. He was about to start back down to the surface when Calla made a sudden move toward the panel.

"What are you doing? Stop!" he yelled.

"Give back my sun!" Calla cried. She started smacking buttons. The lights in the hull went off and on again. Destin could hear the ship's engine trying to deal with the different commands.

"Stop!" Destin said again. "You're going to destroy my ship." He tried to get between Calla and the buttons, but she was strong, and she shoved him away easily.

Then she made a move toward a huge red button. And she was going to push it.

"No!" Destin yelled. "That's the *jump* button!"

Calla held her hand over the button and stared at him. "So?"

Destin's voice shook with fear. "If you press that button, we'll jump right into another sector."

"So?" she said.

"So? I haven't reset the nav system yet. We could jump right into a dying star or a black hole or..."

"Well," she said, her voice calm and cool. "I guess you better give my sun back. Or I'll push it, and we'll both die."

"I told you," Destin said. "I can't."

"Too bad," she said, and with that, she slammed her hand down on the *jump* button.

Destin screamed as his ship leaped through space.

Chapter Four

Destin was still screaming as his ship ended its jump. It came to a stop right next to a giant hunk of space rock. It was so close that the back end of his ship scraped up against it.

"What have you done?" Destin said. He checked his controls. He had to find out where they'd jumped to.

"Oh no," he said. "The nav system is broken. You could have killed us!" he added.

"Like you did my planet?" Calla said.

He turned to her, thinking he was going to tell her off, but then he saw her face. She was crying, and it made her eyes look even more golden. He tried to say something, but there was nothing to say.

She was right. He had killed her planet. Maybe it wasn't dead yet, but it would be soon. And so would everyone on it. He sank down onto the cold metal floor. He tried not to cry, but the memory of the beautiful planet he'd seen put him over the edge. The tears came, and he didn't have the energy to fight them.

Calla shifted from foot to foot and watched him. She didn't seem to know what to make of him crying on the floor.

Destin noticed her feet were bare. He wondered what it was like to walk on the grass of her planet with no boots on. He should have done it while he had the chance.

"Destin," Calla said at last. "Why are you doing this? Tell me why. Give me one good reason."

But he couldn't. "There is none," he said. "It's all pointless. I only do what I'm told. And I hate that about myself. I'm sorry. I wish it was different. But it's all I've ever known."

Calla nodded. "That's what I thought," she said. She paced back and forth for a minute. Finally she stopped and knelt down.

"It's not good enough," she said. "So you're going to find a way to give me back my sun. And I don't care if you say you can't. You're going to find a way."

Destin sighed and wiped his eyes. "Even if I wanted to, I'm not sure it will work. And anyway, you busted my nav system. Thanks for that."

"Oh," she said. She made a move toward the *jump* button again.

"No!" he cried. "Wait! Please stop pressing buttons."

She paused. "What?"

"Let me think," he said. "We can't just go jumping around. We could do that for a thousand years and never get back to your planet. But I have studied the star maps, and I was always good at navigation. If I can figure out where we are now, then we can find our way back. I hope."

He stood and stretched and then called up his star maps. "We need to find a pattern. This could take a while." He set his program to run, but he'd seen it take days to find a match.

Calla stood at the main window.

"What do you see out there?" he asked.

"Nothing," she said in a quiet voice. "Nothing alive."

Destin walked up next to her. His arm brushed hers, and he felt a tiny shock. She moved away a little. He took a little step away too.

Calla was right. There was nothing alive out there. "I've never seen this place before," he said.

They were in a dark place filled with dead planets. They were the leftovers of a war from long ago. Space junk floated by. Bits of old, useless ships.

"Did you kill these planets?" Calla asked. Her voice was shaky.

"Me?" Destin shook his head. "No, I didn't do this."

"But IRIS did?" she asked.

He nodded. "I'm sure of it," he said. IRIS liked to kill things.

"What is the difference between IRIS and you?" Calla asked.

"What?"

"They did this, but you did not. And yet you work for them, killing planets. So aren't *you* IRIS?"

Her eyes dared him to say different, but he could not. She was right. He was IRIS too. Destin looked at the dead planets. Were any of them once his home? For all he knew, this is where he came from. He was working for the corporation that had killed his family. The painful ball was back in his throat again.

"Do you think there is anyone alive out there?" Calla asked in a quiet voice.

Destin shook his head. He swallowed hard. "No way."

"We should look," she said. "There could be someone, right?"

"We won't find anyone," Destin said. "We're all alone. Forever alone."

She backed away from the window. "Is this what will happen to my planet?"

"Yes," he said. His voice was shaky.

"Please, you can't let this happen," she said.

Destin looked at his timekeeper. They only had one day before her sun would die forever, and soon IRIS would come looking for him. He checked his power cells. They were still full. He could return to base or take Calla back. He could not do both. He had to choose, and choose now.

"Will you help me, Destin?" Calla asked.

Chapter Five

Destin stared into Calla's eyes. He couldn't look away even if he wanted to. He felt his heart beat a little faster.

Calla stepped closer to him. "I need you to remember," she said. "Remember a time before IRIS. You have to help me."

She put her hands on his shoulders and squeezed. Destin felt a shock go down his arms and then a warm flush. He could hear Calla inside his mind. *We'll get through it together*, her voice said. A blue lake popped into his mind. And then a feeling of peace. He pulled away.

"W-what was that?" he asked. He was shaking.

But before she could answer, a hail sounded. A Raider ship came up on the radar screen.

"What's that?" Calla asked.

"Nothing good," said Destin. "I have to answer. And you have to hide. Get down."

Calla slid under the control panel.

Destin took a breath. "Raider 1984-225. Destin X here," he said.

A face came onscreen. It was a young

Raider like him. It was Herc. They had gone through training at the same time.

"Hello, Destin," said Herc. "What are you doing way out in the dead zone?"

"Hey, Herc," he said. "I had a little issue with my control panel, but we're working on it."

"We?" Herc asked.

"I, uh, I meant me," said Destin. He felt his face grow hot. He tried to turn things around. "Steal anything good?"

"Oh yeah," Herc said. "I bagged a good one. Nice little planet had a bright sun. Lots of life down there. I have before and after shots, if you want to see. Little planet's all iced up already." Herc laughed.

Destin tried hard not to frown. He couldn't

give his true feelings away. But hearing Herc talk that way made the angry pit in Destin's stomach swirl. He glanced down at Calla. She was crying again.

"Wow," said Destin, forcing a smile. "That's... great."

"Ha!" Herc said with a laugh. "Knew you'd be jealous."

"Well," said Destin, "if there's nothing else, I have to go."

"Happy hunting. Over and out," said Herc. The hail ended.

Destin plunked down into his chair and put his head in his hands.

"Can I come out?" asked Calla.

Destin nodded.

"Are you okay?" she asked.

"No," he said. "I'm not." Seeing Herc had reminded him of who IRIS wanted him to be. But that's not who Destin wanted to be. He was tired of feeling pulled in two.

"Who is Herc? How do you know him?"

"He's from the hub, like me."

"The hub?" she asked.

"It's like a giant prison for orphans, but they call it a training hub. It's where they raise the Raiders. We were all stolen from somewhere. They took us there when we were kids. Kept us in big halls all together. It was always so cold. We were hungry, tired from all the work."

Calla placed her hand on his, and again he got that warm feeling.

Destin thought about those cold nights

in the hub with no sheets on the bunks. All the kids lined up row upon row. At night he'd fallen asleep to the sound of the others crying. Some of them were so young. He couldn't remember his family. All he'd had was the promise of one day flying his own Raider.

At least when was out on his Raider ship, he could gaze out at the stars and see new worlds. Even though he wasn't supposed to visit them, and would never get to live on one, it was a way to dream. A way to keep dreams alive.

"Dreams are rare for you," Calla said, breaking his thoughts.

Destin flinched and yanked his hand

back. "How did you do that? Can you read my mind?"

Calla shook her head. "It's more like...I can feel your feelings. Everyone on my planet can. And others, too, but I don't know if they are alive anymore."

Destin was quiet. He had heard stories like this from some of the kids at the hub, but he'd thought they were making them up. He closed his eyes and took a deep breath. The image of the blue lake flashed in his mind. When he opened his eyes and looked at Calla, he knew what to do. There was no other choice.

He was going to return the energy. Not just to help Calla, but because he needed to do one good thing. His life working for IRIS was empty. From this point on, he was going to make it mean something.

He looked at Calla. "I'm tired of surviving and living for myself. So I'm going to take you home. Back to your people. And I'll fix your sun. Or die trying."

Chapter Six

Destin tried to fix his control panel, but it was no use. He'd known approximately where they were as soon as Herc mentioned the dead zone. But he needed the nav system to properly chart a course. He was not skilled enough to fly without it. Calla was no help because her people had no tech.

They had destroyed it all many years earlier to keep IRIS from finding them.

Finally he decided he would try a reboot. "I'm going to shut the whole thing down and see if that helps," said Destin. He pulled the main power lever, and everything went dark.

Calla stepped a little closer to him.

"It's okay," he said. "We have to wait a bit before turning it back on. It will only be dark for a little while."

He felt her breathing next to him and the warmth of her arm next to his. The backs of their hands brushed.

"Wow," she said.

"Huh?" said Destin.

"Look. The stars."

Destin looked through the main window. Without the ship's inside lights on, it was dark enough that they could see every little star in the galaxy. It was beautiful.

They stood like that longer than they needed to. Destin didn't want it to end. Being next to her, feeling her close, and watching the galaxy float by made him feel the best he ever had. It was like there was a link between them or some special thing that drew them together.

Finally Destin pulled the power lever again. The ship came back to life, beeping and lighting up. His control panel reset.

Almost as soon as it got back online, another hail came through.

Calla ducked down.

Destin pressed the *comms* button. It was Herc again.

"Destin," said Herc. He had a sly smile on his face. "You've been very bad."

"W-what?" Destin asked. Two more Raider ships popped up on his radar screen.

"IRIS sent us all a message saying you went off plan. We have to bring you in."

"No," said Destin. "You can't. I'm heavy with energy here. I can bring it in myself. I told you, it's a glitch in my controls."

Herc laughed. "If you don't let us bring you in, then we have to take your energy and leave you out here in the dead zone."

"No. Oh no," Destin said. Without his nav, he would have to hand fly out of this mess.

"Hey, who is that?" Herc said.

Destin spun around. Calla was standing behind him.

"You will never get this energy!" she yelled. She was so mad that her face had flushed red.

"What the—?" Herc began, but Calla smacked the *comms* button and cut him off.

"He saw you," said Destin. "That means IRIS will know you're here. This is bad."

"I'm sorry," she said. "I couldn't help it."

Destin took a deep breath. "Forget it. I'm done with IRIS. But we have to get out of here. Now."

He put the system into manual flight. "I wish I knew somewhere safe," he said.

An alarm went off. A threat alert. The other Raiders were launching their Star Eaters.

Soon they'd take his energy. They had to leave *now*.

He took Calla's hand and felt the connection between them. "Where?" he asked. "Where would you go?"

The image of the blue lake popped into his mind again.

"My lake," she said. "Back home. Where I can float in peace and all of my cares slide away."

Slide, Destin thought. Float, slide. That was it! "I've got it," he said.

"Where?"

"Somewhere they'll never look. A wormhole I found once. I use it when I want to get somewhere far away fast."

He dialed in the numbers, hoping he'd remembered them correctly. "Now this is going to be fast. I have to hand fly away from them to get clear of this space rubble. And when I tell you, you're going to hit the *jump* button. Okay?"

"Okay," she said.

Destin took the controls and hit the power on full. They zoomed past the line of waiting Raiders and made for an open area away from the dead zone.

The Raiders took off after him, hailing him over and over again. Destin ignored their calls. He flew a wild path, up and down, trying to shake them off.

"I need more speed!" he said. "I'm going

to dump some junk." He flipped a switch and emptied the ship's trash bay behind them. All kinds of garbage hit the Raiders and slowed them a bit.

"They're still coming!" Calla cried.

Destin would need to dump some of his cargo too. Food rations, tools, water tanks—all things needed to survive alone on the ship for a long time. It was important stuff, but it was heavy. The lighter the ship, the faster it would be.

He opened the cargo bay, and it all spilled out. Two Raiders couldn't get around it fast enough. One smashed into a large metal chunk and lost part of its left side. The other bounced off a tank and spun off end over end. There was still one Raider coming after them, and it was fast.

But Destin's ship was faster, and he was a gifted pilot. He'd been first in his training group. They sped out of the dead zone. *Almost there.*

The other Raider bore down on them, nearly ramming the back of his ship.

The threat alarm blared. Too close! They were going to crash.

"Now!" he shouted to Calla as they passed the last bit of space junk.

She slammed her hand down on the *jump* button.

Chapter Seven

The ship hurtled away, leaving the other Raider behind. The stars streaked past them as they hit light speed.

"Hold on!" Destin yelled. "When we hit the wormhole, we're in for a big bump! The quick change in speed is tough on the ship!"

Calla grabbed Destin's arm with one hand and the edge of the panel with the other.

There was a loud bang as they entered the wormhole. They lurched forward as the ship went from top speed to almost a dead stop. Calla fell, but Destin caught her before she could hit the hard floor. They held onto each other for a moment. The rainbow colors of the wormhole swirled around them.

"What is this beauty?" Calla asked. She let go of him and went to the window.

"I found it once on a scouting run. By accident. My ship slipped into it, and I was stuck sliding in it for hours. But it's pretty, and it's a fast way to get where you're going."

"Wait, you said you were in it for hours? We don't have that kind of time."

Destin nodded. "It will seem like hours to us, but when we come out the other side, it will have only been a few minutes."

"Wow," said Calla. "And where will we be when we come out?"

Destin shrugged. "It's different every time. I only know the way in. The way out is a mystery."

"Why is it so pretty?" Calla asked. She took a step back, but her legs wobbled and she sank to her knees. She seemed pale now, like she was losing her healthy color.

"Calla!" Destin hurried to help her. "What is it?"

She put a shaking hand to her head. "I...I've never been this far from home before. And...I'm hungry."

He took her hand. "Yes," Destin said. "You are. And you're tired. I can...feel it."

"You can?" she asked. "That is strange. I thought only people from my planet could do that."

Destin shook his head. "I don't understand anything anymore. But I do know that I'm hungry too. Come on." He helped her up.

They needed to rest and eat. At least they were safe in the wormhole for now.

Destin took her to his tiny galley kitchen and heated up some of the remaining food rations. The brown pucks were mixed with water to form a paste. It didn't taste very good, but it would keep them alive.

"Here," he said, placing the metal bowl in front of her.

She sniffed it and took a tiny taste. She tried to hide the bad face she made.

"It's okay," he said. "I know it's gross."

"I wish you could taste the food from my planet," she said.

They were quiet for a moment. "Eat," Destin said. They both choked down the sludge.

He couldn't help but stare at her. Beautiful wasn't right the right word for Calla. She had all these golden freckles. They went right across her nose and onto her cheeks, kind of in a line. And down her arms too. It reminded him of the stars he gazed at night after night.

But it was her hair he could not stop looking at. It was a curly, white, fluffy mound. It reminded him of wishing flowers. He'd never seen them in real life.

Just once Destin wanted to hold a wishing flower in his hand. He wanted to make a wish and blow the little seeds away on the wind. What were those flowers called again? He couldn't remember, but that's what she reminded him of.

"A wild wishing flower," he said out loud without meaning to.

"What?" she asked.

"You," he said. "You remind me of that wild-flower, the one you can wish on."

She smiled, and then it turned into a yawn.

"You need to rest," said Destin. He showed her to his cramped sleeping bunk. "You can sleep for a while, and I'll figure out our next move."

"Wait," she said. "Tell me about these." She pointed to a bunch of pictures he'd put on his wall.

"Oh," he said. "Those are just places I always wanted to go to." They were pictures of mountains and lakes. Pictures that looked like a dream. More stuff IRIS didn't allow. Pictures and dreaming.

"It looks like my home," Calla said. "Do you remember yours?"

Destin sat on the bed and let out a sigh. "This is my home," he said, pointing to his ship. "It's the only place I ever had to myself."

It meant everything to have his own Raider ship to explore the far reaches of space. He may not have loved stealing energy, but he did love spying on new worlds. Every time found a new one, he had the same thought. *Is this where I came from?* But he knew the answer was always no, because IRIS had killed his home planet.

Calla leaned toward him and put her arms around him.

"What are you doing?" he asked. He didn't know what to do. "What is this?"

"A hug," she said. "You need one."

He felt the warmth of her hug and relaxed into it. No one had ever given him one before. It was like all his feelings were flowing into her, and hers into him.

Chapter Eight

Destin awoke when his ship rattled and bumped. He sat up, blinking. At first he didn't know where he was, and then he saw Calla sleeping on the bunk next to him. He checked his timekeeper. It had been five hours. They must have gone all the way through the wormhole.

"Calla," he said. He touched her shoulder softly.

She opened her golden eyes and smiled.

"We're here," he said.

"Where?" she asked.

"Let's see," he said.

They went to the controls and looked out the window. Yes, Destin had been to this sector before. He was happy to see moons and star patterns that he recognized. He could use them to work out the way back to Calla's planet. He plotted his trip into his star map, and it showed him where to go. They weren't that far away. He could get there in one short jump. Something was actually working out.

Then he noticed there were a bunch of missed hails. All from Captain Juno. He clicked on a recorded message. Juno's face popped up onscreen, but her voice was fuzzy and hard to hear. There was one phrase he understood loud and clear though.

"You will never be free," she said. "You belong to IRIS."

Calla came up behind him and switched it off. "I don't like her," she said.

Destin smiled a sad smile. "But she's right. I will never be free, not until I let go of this ship."

Calla took his hand. "Then you will come home with me. To stay."

Home, Destin thought. Could he?

"I...would have to destroy my ship after we return the energy," he said. "Otherwise they'd be able to track it."

"Would you do that?" she asked.

He nodded. "Yes," he said. "I would. And I know what to do about IRIS. I have a plan. Are you a good liar?"

Calla grinned. "I can try."

Destin had Calla record a message to IRIS saying that she had taken over the ship. That Destin was dead and now she was going to blow up the ship.

Destin made sure to send the comm to IRIS with fake call numbers to throw them off. They would track him, and find him, but this would make it take longer, and by then the ship would be gone. There would be nothing to find but space dust.

Destin set a new course based on his star map. "This is it, I think," he said. "Does this look right?"

"I'm not sure," Calla said. "But I believe in you."

Destin smiled. "Do you want to push the button?" he asked.

She smiled. "I like doing that," she said.

"Yeah, I know."

"You know, it's still a big risk," she said. "IRIS could still find us and kill us all."

"Yes," he said. "But there's a lot of planets out there. A lot of stars. Better to take my chances. I'd rather die than live alone for the rest of my life."

She took his hand and then hit the button.

Chapter Nine

The jump brought them back to the place where they'd met, high above Calla's planet. Their joy didn't last long. Calla's planet was hurting. There were bad storms forming on the surface, and the sun was dimming fast.

"Oh no," she cried. "Are we too late?"

"Not if I can help it," he said. He powered

on the Star Eater. It hummed and pulled out its long arm. The eye opened up.

"That is so scary," Calla said.

"My feelings exactly," said Destin. He paused before switching the Star Eater into reverse mode. He'd never done it before. He'd only ever heard about it. And what he'd heard was that it was very dangerous. His ship could blow up, or the sun could blow up and kill everything in the system.

"Calla," he said. "You have to return to the surface first."

"What do you mean?" she asked.

"It's too dangerous for you to be on board. There's a very real chance I will die doing this, and I can't risk your life. I've already done that, and I won't ever do it again."

Calla shook her head. "No! We do this together."

"Calla, you have to trust me," he said.

"I do," she said. She touched his face. "I know what you feel in your heart. But I won't let you do it alone."

Destin took a deep breath. He would not be able to get her to agree. "Then hang on," he said.

He punched the Star Eater into reverse mode and backed away.

A high screech came from the Star Eater as it shot pure energy from its eye back into the dying sun.

The ship rumbled and swayed and shook. Screws on the walls and floors came loose. The metal panels sagged inward. It seemed like the ship was going to fall apart any second.

"Destin!" Calla grabbed him.

They huddled together on the floor and watched as the sun grew brighter and brighter. A blinding flash of light filled the ship. They covered their eyes and held each other close.

Destin kept waiting for them to blow up or be burned alive. Being so close to Calla, with his cheek pressed against hers, he almost didn't care.

Finally it was over, and the Star Eater

hummed to a close. The ship went dark. There was only enough power left to run the main systems.

"We did it," Calla said. "My sun, my planet. They live."

"Now let's finish it," he said.

There was nothing left to do except destroy his ship. Destin set the self-destruct command. He said goodbye to the only life he'd ever known. He took nothing except those few old books he had hidden. The warning system started counting down.

They climbed into the single eject pod with a few minutes to spare. It was a tight fit. Destin set the flight path to the surface. One last trip, and he'd be on the surface again with Calla. On a real planet. A place that could be home. He might always fear IRIS finding them, but it was worth it to try.

Destin wrapped his arms around Calla.

"You sure you want me to come?" he asked.

Calla laughed. "It's a little bit late now, don't you think?"

The threat system counted down. *ONE MINUTE TO LAUNCH.*

She leaned in closer to him and brushed her lips against his.

"Want to hit the button?" he asked when he could breathe again.

Of course she did.

Chapter Ten

They landed safely, then smashed and burned all the tech in the escape pod. Later they filled the body of the pod with dirt and grew food in it. Destin liked to look at it and remember where he came from. It made him even happier to be on this new planet.

He had a new life there. New friends. And, of course, Calla. All were welcoming to him, even though he had almost killed them. They understood, having lived under the threat of IRIS for so long. Together they worked to build a new future. It was as if Destin had always belonged to them, and them to him.

It was a dream to be on a real planet with water and trees and mountains. It was a dream to have someone in his life who maybe, probably, loved him. It was a dream to have someone he could love back. The feeling of the sun on his face every day was everything.

One warm morning Calla woke him up

from a nap by the lake. He opened his eyes to the sky. She was leaning over him, the sun a halo around her white hair.

"I have a surprise for you," she said. "Something I want you to see."

They went for a long walk through the trees. When they came out on the other side, the sun was shining down on a field of wishing flowers.

Calla walked out into the field and smiled. She picked a fluffy white flower. "Here," she said. She handed it to him.

He took it and closed his eyes. He made a wish. It was the only wish he'd ever made. He hoped it would keep coming true.

Acknowledgments

I'd like to thank the forests, rivers, mountains and lakes I visited while writing this book, as well as the people who maintain and protect our green spaces and wildlife. I spent time viewing the outdoors from the back of a canoe, my face in the sun, just listening to the world. It was nice to be away from the usual noise of social media, and far from the pollution that keeps us from seeing the stars at night. When everything is overwhelming, and we're locked down and disconnected, it's healing to get outside. Touch a flower. Stand in the grass. Walk in the rain. Float on a lake. Make a wish on a dandelion. As always, my family and friends are the inspiration for

every book I write. This one is for my kids—
two amazing people who love being outside.
They never met a stump or a worm or a rock
or a stream they didn't like. I hope they never
lose that. Thank you to everyone at Orca for
all that you do, for a chance to write this
book with you and for your commitment to
environmentally conscious books for youth.
You're the best.

Brooke Carter is a Canadian novelist and the author of several contemporary books for teens, including *Double or Nothing* (Junior Library Guild Gold Selection), *Learning Seventeen* (CCBC Best Book for Teens) and *Sulfur Heart* from the Orca Soundings line. She earned her MFA in creative writing at the University of British Columbia.